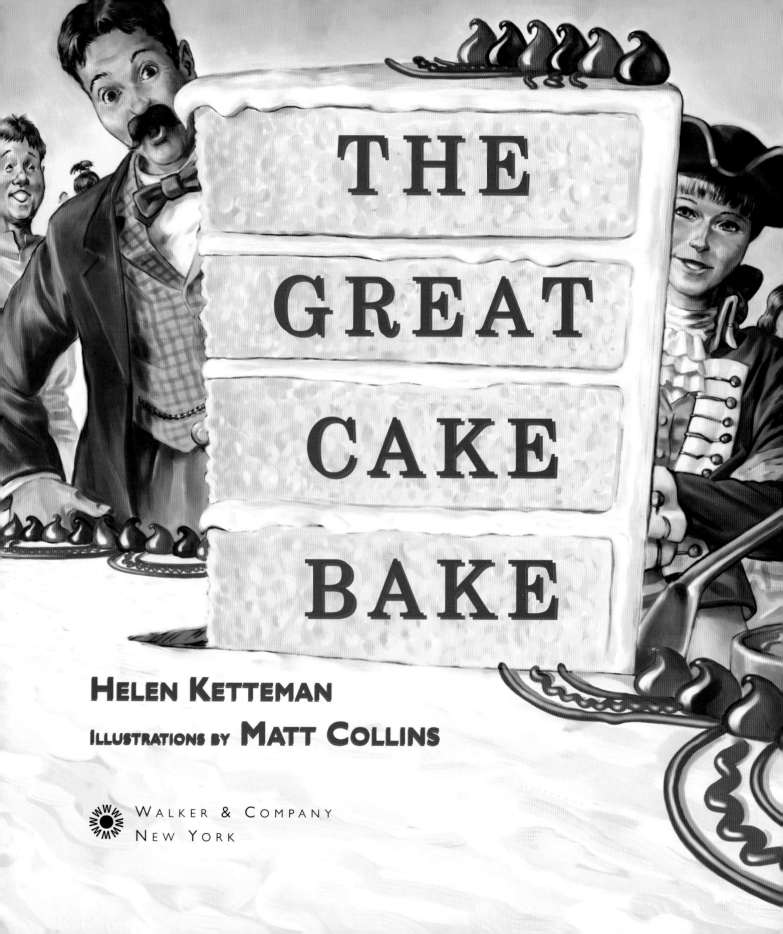

THE GREAT CAKE BAKE

Helen Ketteman

Illustrations by Matt Collins

Walker & Company
New York

To my grandnephews and grandnieces:
Madison Kelley; Kathleen and Jesse Reynolds; Caylee Comer;
and Brandi, Cameron, Trey, and Jacob Winslow Paschal.
And to the grand-cats and grand-dogs as well.
—H. K.

For Amy.
—M. C.

First published in the United States of America in 2005 by Walker Publishing Company, Inc.

Published simultaneously in Canada by Fitzhenry and Whiteside, Markham, Ontario L3R 4T8

For information about permission to reproduce selections from this book,
write to Permissions, Walker & Company, 104 Fifth Avenue, New York, New York 10011

Library of Congress Cataloging-in-Publication Data

Ketteman, Helen.
The great cake bake / Helen Ketteman ; illustrations by Matt Collins.
p. cm.
Summary: When her town hosts a Fourth of July cake competition, Donna Rae tries to bake
the best cake ever, but with every patriotic confection she makes something goes wrong.
ISBN 0-8027-8950-1 (HC) — ISBN 0-8027-8952-8 (RE)
[1. Baking—Fiction. 2. Contests—Fiction. 3. Fourth of July—Fiction.] I. Collins, Matt, ill. II. Title.

PZ7.K494Gr 2005
[E]—dc22
2004055486

The illustrations for this book were created using PRISMACOLOR pencils and Painter 8.

Book design by Diane Hobbing of Snap-Haus Graphics

Visit Walker & Company's Web site at www.walkeryoungreaders.com

Printed in Hong Kong

2 4 6 8 10 9 7 5 3 1

It was all the mayor's fault. He announced the great cake bake to be held at Danville's Fourth of July celebration too early, which gave Donna Rae Hadley extra time to think. And that meant trouble. Donna Rae was crazy about contests. And she was known for going a bit too far.

Last year, during the final judging of the Easter bonnet contest, the live bunny on Donna Rae's bonnet got wind of the fresh alfalfa nest of Easter eggs on Pearl Hawkins's bonnet. In a lightning-quick move, the bunny hopped right onto Pearl's hat and started chewing.

Easter eggs flew everywhere, and Donna Rae was thrown out of the contest on the grounds

that her hat ate the competition.

Pearl was awarded first place,
but she never quite forgave Donna Rae.

So when Donna Rae learned of the great cake bake, she thought of a brilliant Boston Tea Party cake that would serve the judges cake and tea together.

She covered a piece of plywood with foil, rigged a fountain on the platform, then set a punch bowl next to it. She decided to do a test run.

Donna Rae baked sheets and sheets of cake. She constructed cake buildings, cake piers, and a cake ocean, all nestled around the fountain and punch bowl.

"Mayor Fargenberg has to see this!" She invited him over.

The mayor came right away. He was sweet on Donna Rae, though she hadn't noticed. When he saw her creation, his eyes widened.

"Such a cake!" he exclaimed.

Donna Rae placed a chair beside the cake.

"Have a seat, Alfred. There's a surprise."

Donna Rae cleared her throat. "Tea is served!" She pressed a button. *Whirrrrr.* Nothing happened.

"Must be clogged," said Donna Rae. She pressed harder. Nothing. The mayor leaned closer to take a look.

Donna Rae jabbed the button again. *SPLOOOSH!!* Tea spewed everywhere.

The mayor mopped his face. "Try making a cake that won't drown the judges!" He went home to change his clothes.

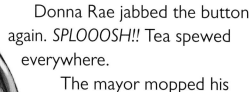

"I'll try something different," said Donna Rae. She thought about the Statue of Liberty, a gift from the people of France to honor the one-hundredth birthday of America's Declaration of Independence. What could be better for the Fourth of July than a Statue of Liberty cake?

Donna Rae welded a few pipes and connected them to the tank from her gas barbecue grill. "Time for a test run," she said.

Donna Rae
baked sheets and
sheets of cake.

She covered the
tubes with foil, then
constructed the
Statue of Liberty
around them.

Only the top of one tube
poked out of Lady Liberty's
torch. She called the mayor
to come see.

"Beautiful!" he declared.

"There's a surprise," said Donna Rae. She handed the mayor a match. "Will you do the honor of lighting Lady Liberty's torch?" The mayor struck a match. Donna Rae turned a valve.

When the smoke cleared, the mayor wiped his face. "My mustache! It's . . . gone! No more exploding cakes! It's dangerous. Besides, I . . . I'd miss you if you blew yourself to bits."

Donna Rae blushed. "Why Alfred, I didn't know you cared. You know, you look quite handsome without that scruffy mustache."

The mayor grinned, then stuttered, "I . . . I'd better go clean up."

Donna Rae rethought her project. "Paul Revere's ride would make the best cake of all!" The contest was tomorrow. There'd be no time for a test run, but this cake's surprise had nothing to squirt, nothing to explode. Nothing would go wrong.

Donna Rae worked all night long. She enlarged the platform and baked enough cake to build the entire town of Boston on an extrawide cobblestone street. She finished just as the sun rose. Her cake was gigantic, the most spectacular one she'd ever seen!

Donna Rae dressed as Paul Revere and looked in the mirror. She felt a rush of pride. Her cousin Will helped load the cake onto his truck. His horse, Chester, trotted behind.

When they got to city hall, the whole town was there. Two long cake-filled tables sat across from each other. Donna Rae and Will set her cake between them. People crowded around.

When the judges approached Donna Rae's cake, she held up her hand. "There's a surprise with my cake."

Mayor Fargenberg turned white.

"Don't worry," Donna Rae whispered.

Donna Rae grabbed Chester's reins. The crowd gasped. Donna Rae mounted the horse. The crowd held its breath as Chester stepped onto the cobblestone street that led up to Donna Rae's cake.

"The British are coming!" Donna Rae shouted. In her excitement, she pulled the reins a little too tight. Chester's head jerked back.

He stumbled off the road and crushed the Old North Church. He skidded off the cake, knocking over one of the tables.

Donna Rae hit the other table. Cakes flew faster than double-struck lightning.

No one knows for sure who threw the first handful of cake.

Some say it was Pearl, taking aim at Donna Rae.

But when it was all over, everyone was covered with cake.

Mayor Fargenberg was blamed for the whole mess. He would have been voted out of office in the next election, but he made two announcements later that day that saved him.

The first announcement was that there would be another cake bake the next Fourth of July. The second announcement was that Donna Rae had agreed to be his bride. Of course, as the mayor's wife, she would not be eligible to enter. Instead, she would be a judge. Everyone cheered.

Donna Rae wouldn't mind missing the contest. After all, she had a wedding to plan. She wanted her wedding cake to be one Danville would always remember.

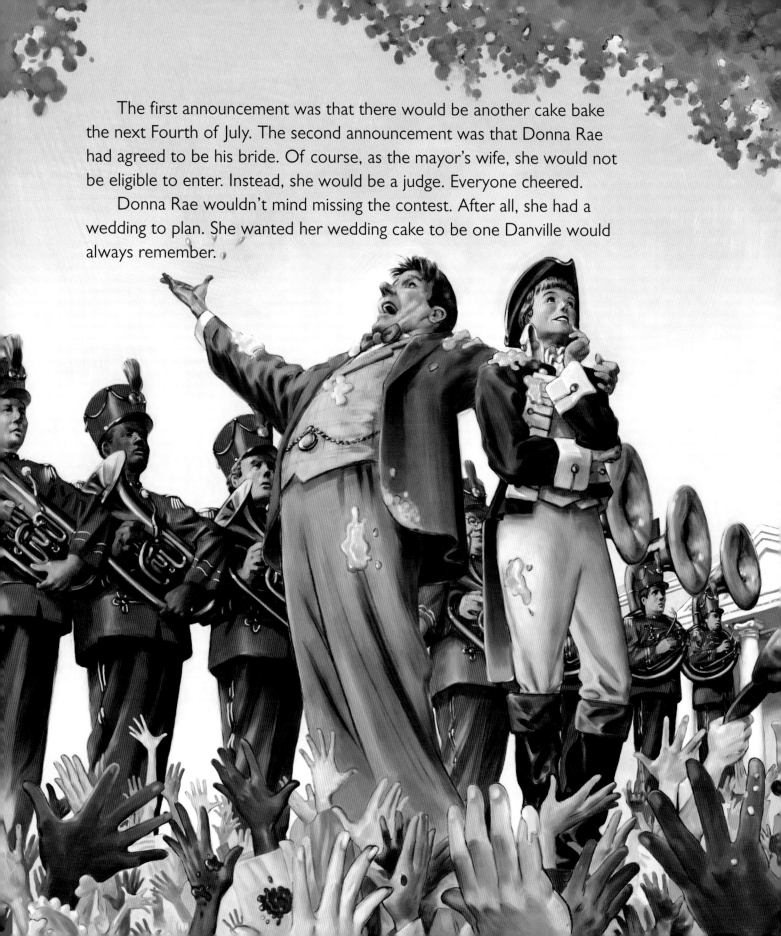